A

MW01488958

When the Horses are Gone

A Story of the Nez Perce Indian Tribe

by Alan Venable

Don Johnston Incorporated
Volo, Illinois

About the Reader

Jim DeNomie is a member of the Bad River Band of Chippewa Indians of Lake Superior in Wisconsin. He visits schools to give talks about Native American culture and about the Native Americans who live near the Western Great Lakes. Jim is the Host and Co-Producer of a radio program about Native Americans called *Voices from the Circle*. This program is available on the internet at www.airos.org, and on the American Indian Radio On Satellite (AIROS) network. Jim works on social justice issues for Native Americans and other minority groups.

Chapter 1

Gray Fox Comes Home

"The first white men of your people who came to our country were named Lewis and Clark. They brought many things which our people had never seen. They talked straight and our people gave them a great feast as proof that their hearts were friendly. All the Nez Perce made friends with Lewis and Clark and agreed to let them pass through their country and never to make war on white men. This promise the Nez Perce have never broken."

— Chief Joseph (Rolling Thunder)
Hin-mah-too-yah-lat-kekt
(1840-1904)

It was the summer of 1863. Gray Fox had just returned to his village. He was an Indian of the Nez Perce tribe. The Nez Perce Indians lived on land that is now part of Idaho and Oregon.

Gray Fox had gone east with ten other men to hunt buffalo on the plains. They had been away for many months.

Gray Fox had brought back some thick buffalo robes to keep his family warm in the winter. He had also brought back a fine gray horse.

This new horse was strong. It held its head up high and proud as Gray Fox rode into the village.

Gray Fox was glad to see his wife again after such a long time away. Their new baby son had just been born. Gray Fox asked his wife to bring the baby outside. Gray Fox showed them his fine new horse.

"The baby needs a name," said Gray Fox. "We will call him 'Little Proud Horse,' " he said.

Gray Fox was happy to see his family, but he was also worried.

Gray Fox had been hearing bad news and rumors about the white men who were coming from the east.

For many years, white people had been coming onto Nez Perce land. These people called themselves Americans. At first, they had just passed through the Nez Perce land with their horses and wagons and cattle as they traveled west to Oregon. But then they had begun to stay on the Nez Perce land. They were trying to steal the land and keep it for themselves.

In 1855, the chiefs from the Nez Perce tribe had met with the white leaders from Oregon to talk about the problem. The Americans had asked the chiefs to make a deal. The Americans wanted the chiefs to sign a treaty.

The white leaders had explained the treaty to the chiefs. "If you and your tribe agree to give us half of your land, then we will leave the rest of the Nez Perce land alone. Our soldiers will protect your land and it will belong to your people forever," the white leaders had promised.

The chiefs had been angry because the Americans were stealing their land. But the chiefs also knew that there were many thousands of Americans and there were only about 6,000 Nez Perce. No other tribe had ever beaten the Americans in a war. So the chiefs had agreed to the treaty. They gave away half of their land. They hoped that the treaty would bring peace that would last a long time.

But the peace had not lasted for long.

A few years later, white men had found gold on the Nez Perce land, and now white miners were coming onto the land to steal the gold.

So the chiefs of the Nez Perce complained to the leaders of the Americans. "We have lived in peace with you for many years," they said. "When your people crossed our land in wagons, we helped them find their way. Even when they brought the white man's sickness to our people, we did not hurt them.

When a white man kills a Nez Perce, we do not fight back and kill one of your men," the chiefs said. "We do not take revenge. But now white men have come to take gold from our land. We don't want to kill these men. Where are the soldiers who were supposed to protect our lands? You promised that you would send them to us," the chiefs said.

But the Americans broke their promise. "Our soldiers cannot keep the miners off your land," they said. "Our soldiers cannot force our people to follow the treaty."

Chapter 2

The New Treaty

"For a short time we lived quietly. But this could not last. White men had found gold in the mountains around the land of the Winding Water. When the white men were few and we were strong, we could have killed them off, but the Nez Perce wishes to live at peace."

— Chief Joseph (Rolling Thunder)
Hin-mah-too-yah-lat-kekt

When Gray Fox heard these stories, he went to see his friend, Rolling Thunder. Rolling Thunder was the son of the old chief. The whites called the old chief the name Chief Joseph. They gave Rolling Thunder the name Young Joseph. They did not bother to learn the real names of the Indians.

"What has happened here while I was gone?" Gray Fox asked Rolling Thunder.

"The news is bad," said Rolling Thunder. "The white soldiers will not protect us from the miners.

The white leaders want us to sign a new treaty instead. They want to take away more of our land," said Rolling Thunder.

"How much more?" asked Gray Fox.

Rolling Thunder held up his hand. He said, "Pretend that my hand is the land of our fathers." Then he pointed to just the tip of his thumb. "This is how much of our land they would let us keep. The whites call this small piece of land a reservation. We would not be allowed to live anywhere else," he said.

CANADA

UNITED STATES

Washington

Montana

Nez Perce land by 1863

Nez Perce land in 1855

Oregon

Idaho

Gray Fox was angry. "They will force us to become farmers like the white men," he shouted. "And the Nez Perce are not farmers! In the spring we go down to our rivers to fish for salmon. In the summer we move our village up to our meadows so that our women can gather food there. In the summer we bring our horses up into our high valley in the mountains so that they can eat grass and grow strong for the winter. We must always have our horses for hunting," continued Gray Fox.

"And in the winter we must leave the mountains and go down into the canyons where the air is warmer and the snow is not deep," said Gray Fox. "How can we live on a tiny scrap of land!"

Rolling Thunder answered, "The whites do not care how we live. The whites are hungry for more of our land."

"The white men do not care about us at all," said Gray Fox bitterly. "And what about the valley where we have our village? Will this valley be part of the reservation?" he asked.

"No," answered Rolling Thunder.

Now Gray Fox was furious. "We cannot agree to this," he said. "We can never give away our beautiful valley to the white men!"

"Some of the other Nez Perce chiefs have already given away their valleys," said Rolling Thunder. "They have moved their villages onto the new reservation. But there are other chiefs who are like my father. They have all promised that we will never leave our valleys."

"Your father, Chief Joseph, is old," said Gray Fox. "You may become the leader of our village when he dies. What will you do then?" asked Gray Fox.

"I will never sign the treaty," Rolling Thunder promised.

Gray Fox was glad to hear this from his friend. Rolling Thunder had never led the people of the village in a battle. He had never gone with Gray Fox on the long hunt for buffalo. But Gray Fox knew that Rolling Thunder was as brave as any warrior in the Nez Perce tribe.

Chapter 3

Proud Horse Grows Up

"We were like deer. The white men were like grizzly bears. We had a small country. Their country was large. We were contented to let things remain as the Great Spirit Chief made them. They were not."

> — Chief Joseph (Rolling Thunder)
> Hin-mah-too-yah-lat-kekt

The years went by and old Chief Joseph was close to death. Just before he died, he spoke to his son, Rolling Thunder. "The bones of my father are buried in this valley," said the Chief. "Soon you will bury me here. This valley will always be our mother. When you are chief, you must keep our people in this valley," said Chief Joseph. "This is our land forever."

Rolling Thunder said, "I promise that we will never leave this valley."

So the village of Gray Fox and Rolling Thunder stayed in the valley, far away from the tiny new reservation. Some of the other villages stayed off the reservation, too.

As each year passed, Gray Fox watched his son, Proud Horse, grow bigger. Soon, Proud Horse began to take care of his father's horses. His family had 20 horses, and Proud Horse learned about each one the way a father knows about his children. Some horses were for riding. Other horses were for carrying the teepee and food.

A teepee was like a tall tent that was made out of wooden poles and animal skins.

Sometimes in the summer, Proud Horse went hunting with his father. Other times Proud Horse stayed behind to take care of the horses. When Gray Fox came back from hunting, he would ask Proud Horse about the young colts. If the colts were safe, he would say to Proud Horse, "You have done well. Without our horses, we would be like a man who has no legs. We cannot live without our horses."

But more and more whites came into the valley. When Proud Horse found the white men's cattle in the same meadow with his family's horses, he would throw stones to chase the cattle away. Sometimes he would find a white man in the meadow, cutting the grass to take it back to his ranch. Proud Horse would stare at the white man to show that he was angry, but the man would only laugh at him and go on cutting the grass.

Every year, more of the Nez Perce were attacked by white men.

Sometimes Proud Horse would find a white man in the meadow, cutting the grass to take it back to his ranch.

The Nez Perce were learning that American laws were unfair. If an American man killed a Nez Perce man, the American was never punished. But if an Indian killed a white man, the soldiers would come and hang the Indian.

Soon the whites had killed 30 Nez Perce, but the Nez Perce had never killed a single white man. The chiefs kept saying, "Keep the peace. Do not take revenge. Remember that the white man's army is strong."

The Americans had built a fort on the Nez Perce reservation. The fort had high walls to protect the soldiers from the Indians. The leader at the fort was a man called General Howard.

It was the month of May and the valleys were green. The Nez Perce were camping in the meadows while the chiefs were meeting with General Howard at the fort. Once again, he was telling them that they had to move onto the reservation.

Chapter 4

No Other Choice

"Let me be a free man, free to think and talk and act for myself. I am not a child. I think for myself. No one else can think for me."

> — Chief Joseph (Rolling Thunder)
> Hin-mah-too-yah-lat-kekt

Proud Horse thought he knew what the chiefs would say to General Howard. "The chiefs will tell the General that we will never leave our mountains and valleys," said Proud Horse to himself. "We will never leave our rivers and meadows. We will never live on the reservation."

But when Rolling Thunder came back from the fort, he said that General Howard would not listen. "He tied up our leader and put him in a cage like an animal," said Rolling Thunder. "Then he ordered us to go onto the reservation.

General Howard said that he will order his soldiers to make us go to the reservation if we do not go there by ourselves," said Rolling Thunder.

"Look at us," he continued. "We have only a few hundred men. The general can get thousands of soldiers. His soldiers have better guns. We cannot stop them. So we must do as they say."

The young men were angry. "We will never give up our valley," they said. We would rather die fighting."

But Rolling Thunder said, "The army has given us 30 days to move onto the reservation. I cannot make you go with me, but I will go. So if you want to stay here and be free, then you will have to choose someone else to lead your war against the whites."

Proud Horse went to his father, Gray Fox. "I will become a warrior now," said Proud Horse. "I will fight beside you to stay in our valley."

Gray Fox was proud of his son, but he said, "No, son. Rolling Thunder is right.

We have no choice," said Gray Fox. "We must go onto the reservation."

Gray Fox saw that Proud Horse was angry. "I am not acting like a coward," said Gray Fox. "If I did not have a family, I would fight the white men now. I must protect my family. The whites would kill our women and children. That is why we must go onto the reservation," Gray Fox explained.

Finally everyone in the village agreed to go onto the reservation. Even Proud Horse agreed to go, but he could not help feeling angry.

There were 600 people leaving the valley. Everyone helped to pack up the teepees. Then the men gathered the horses into one big herd. There were more than 1,000 horses! Proud Horse had never seen so many horses all together.

The reservation was 100 miles away. The people walked quickly until they came to the Snake River. The snow was still melting in the mountains and running down into the rivers, so the Snake River was deep and cold and the water was moving fast. The horses were afraid to cross.

"We must chase the horses into the river," Gray Fox told Proud Horse. Gray Fox and Proud Horse took their horses behind the rest of the herd. Proud Horse and his father shouted and then galloped into the herd until all of the horses started running. When the horses reached the river, they were moving so fast that they pushed each other into the rushing water. Soon most of them were safe on the other side. But hundreds of other horses drowned or were swept far downstream where they could be stolen by white men.

Some of the people crossed the river on the backs of the horses. Others went across in small boats that they had made from buffalo skins.

When Proud Horse got to the other side of the river, he looked for his colts. Seven colts had been born that spring, and now all of them had drowned. Proud Horse was ashamed that his colts had died.

But Gray Fox said to him, "It is not your fault, my son. The General made us cross this river while it was too dangerous.

Next spring, our horses will have new colts on the reservation," said Gray Fox.

In a few days, they were near the reservation. "It is not time for us to go there yet," Rolling Thunder told the warriors. "More Nez Perce people are coming from the other valleys. We will wait for them here in this meadow. We can live as free people for a few more days," he said.

They tried to be happy. They ate together. They raced their horses.

They played their drums and danced and sang because they were proud to be Nez Perce. But now and then the whole camp became silent and angry as they thought about the white men.

Chapter 5

Revenge

"The earth is the mother of all people, and all people should have equal rights upon it."

— Chief Joseph (Rolling Thunder)
Hin-mah-too-yah-lat-kekt

The older men in the tribe decided to have a parade in the meadow. They rode their horses around the teepees and shouted about how brave they had been in buffalo hunts and in battles with other tribes.

Two young men joined the parade. They rode together on one horse, but they acted like they were warriors, also. The older men laughed at them for showing off.

The old men made fun of one of the young men.

"A white man killed your father, but you never punished him," said the old men. "You did not get revenge for the death of your father. You must be a coward," they shouted.

But the young man knew that he was not a coward. He had not gotten revenge because his dying father had made him promise not to do it.

That night the young man could not stop thinking about how the older men had made fun of him. After everyone was asleep, he and two of his friends rode off in the darkness.

The next morning Proud Horse saw the young men come back into camp. They were riding new horses and they were carrying new guns.

One of them said, "White men have stolen our lands and killed our people. So we have just killed four white men and taken their horses and guns."

The other young men in the village cheered. Then some of them got onto their horses and rode out to kill more whites. Proud Horse wanted to go with them, but Gray Fox stopped him.

One of the young men said, "White men have stolen our lands and killed our people. So we have just killed four white men and taken their horses and guns."

"They are doing a foolish thing," said Gray Fox. "Now everyone in our tribe will suffer for this."

Quickly, everyone in the camp began to pack up the teepees. The chiefs sent a warrior to the reservation to speak to the Nez Perce who were living there. "Tell the Nez Perce about the killings. Tell them that there is danger. Tell them that we are coming to join them as quickly as we can," the chiefs said.

But the Nez Perce who were already on the reservation didn't want the others to come. They knew that the soldiers would come looking for the people from the camp. "If your village comes onto the reservation now, the soldiers will follow you and kill us," said a chief from the reservation. "Go back to the meadow and tell the people that they must not come here. They must go somewhere else."

Rolling Thunder decided to lead the people to a place near the reservation. It was a place where they could defend themselves.

"There is only one way that the soldiers can find us here," Rolling Thunder told his people. He pointed at a long, steep hill. "The soldiers must ride their horses down that hill into our camp. There are no trees on the hill, so it will be easy for us to see the soldiers if they try to attack us," he explained.

At the new camp, the Nez Perce waited for the soldiers. If General Howard came with them, Rolling Thunder planned to tell him what had happened.

"I will ask the General to let us go onto the reservation without any more fighting," said Rolling Thunder. "But I do not know what the General will say, so we must be ready to fight."

"There are only 70 of us," Gray Fox said. "And we only have 50 guns. And most of our guns are not as good as the soldiers' guns."

Rolling Thunder gave one of the best guns to Gray Fox. Many warriors would only have bows or spears.

Proud Horse wanted to fight, but Gray Fox said, "No, my son. You must stay and guard the horses. If there is a battle, the soldiers might try to steal our horses. Then our people will be helpless."

Chapter 6

The First Big Battle

"Whenever the white man treats the Indian as they treat each other, then we shall have no more wars. We shall be all alike — brothers of one father and mother, with one sky above us and one country around us and one government for all."

> — Chief Joseph (Rolling Thunder)
> Hin-mah-too-yah-lat-kekt

The next morning, the warriors found places to hide behind small hills where the American soldiers could not see them. Proud Horse took most of the horses to a safe place behind the camp to guard them.

As the sun rose higher, Proud Horse could see more than 100 American soldiers coming down the long hill. Each of the soldiers was carrying a rifle. They were spread out in a wide line. One of the soldiers had a horn that was called a bugle. He was called the bugler.

The Nez Perce noticed that the leader of the soldiers was giving commands to the bugler. Every time the leader gave a command, the bugler would blow the horn. The notes that he played told the soldiers what to do.

A few of the Nez Perce warriors rode slowly up the hill toward the soldiers. The warriors were carrying a white flag to show that they wanted to talk with General Howard in peace. But the General wasn't there. He had sent another man to lead the soldiers.

Suddenly one of the Americans began to shoot at the Nez Perce warriors. The warriors quickly turned their horses around and rode back down the hill.

Then Gray Fox carefully aimed his gun and pulled the trigger. His shot rang out, and the soldier with the bugle fell to the ground and died. "There!" thought Gray Fox. "Now the soldiers won't know what to do."

Then everyone began to shoot. Some of the warriors came out of their hiding places and began to attack the soldiers from every side.

When the Horses are Gone
A Story of the Nez Perce Indian Tribe

The soldiers' horses were tired and slow because they had been walking all night. But the Nez Perce horses were fresh and fast.

Many other warriors stayed hidden and shot at the soldiers while the soldiers rode around in the open. In a short time, 33 American soldiers lay dead on the ground, but all the Nez Perce were still alive. The rest of the soldiers rode back to the fort.

"We are still free!" exclaimed Gray Fox.

The warriors picked up the guns that the soldiers had left behind. There were 63 guns! Now the Nez Perce had guns that were as good as the guns of the army.

The young warriors felt strong and powerful. "Let the soldiers come again!" they shouted. "We will kill more of them!"

But the chiefs knew better. They knew that the army would come again. "The next time, the soldiers will bring even bigger guns," said the chiefs. "They will bring cannons, and they will bring many more soldiers."

When General Howard learned that an American had started the shooting, he was angry. But he decided that there was only one thing to do. "We will get more soldiers," he told his men. "And we will go after the Nez Perce."

Soon the fort was filled with hundreds of soldiers from other forts. When other white men heard the news, they also came to the fort. These men were not soldiers, but they wanted to join the fight.

General Howard began to collect wagons and mules to carry food and supplies for his army. Then he hired Indians from other tribes. "You will be my scouts," he told them. "You know these mountains better than my soldiers, so you can help us follow the Nez Perce."

Chapter 7

Into Montana

"Good words do not give me back my children. Good words will not give my people a home where they can live in peace and take care of themselves. I am tired of talk that comes to nothing. It makes my heart sick when I remember all the good words and all the broken promises. There has been too much talking by men who had no right to talk."

> — Chief Joseph (Rolling Thunder)
> Hin-mah-too-yah-lat-kekt

It was almost the end of June 1877.
General Howard sent some of his
men to a Nez Perce village on the
reservation. The leader of this village
was a chief named Looking Glass.
The General wanted to make sure that
Looking Glass didn't help Rolling
Thunder's people in their battle.

General Howard had told his
soldiers not to use their guns when
they went to the village. But one of
the soldiers began to shoot. Then all
the soldiers started shooting and
rushed into the village.

The Nez Perce people did not know why the soldiers were attacking them. Mothers grabbed their children and ran out of the village and up into the hills. The warriors led the horses into the hills, also. From there, they watched the soldiers burn their teepees. Then Looking Glass led his village to join Rolling Thunder and his people.

"You are the only Nez Perce who are free now," Looking Glass told Rolling Thunder. "We will join you in your fight against the whites."

Soon other Nez Perce Indians joined them from the reservation. They all knew that Rolling Thunder was not really a war chief. He could run the camp. He could get the people to work together and to travel quickly. But Looking Glass was a war chief. He had fought other tribes in Montana. He could lead the Nez Perce in battle.

Now the Nez Perce had more than 200 warriors and more than 2,000 horses. But there were also 500 women, children and old men who could not fight anymore. The warriors would have to protect these people.

The chiefs met with their men to decide what to do next. They didn't think that General Howard would let them go onto the reservation any longer. They had to move quickly because they knew that the army would come back.

The Nez Perce decided to cross the Rocky Mountains into Montana. On the buffalo plains, they would find their old friends, the Crow tribe. They would ask the Crow people to join their fight. Or perhaps the army would not bother to follow them over the mountains.

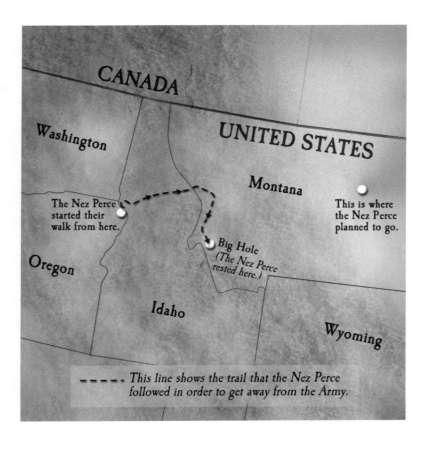

CANADA

Washington

UNITED STATES

Montana

The Nez Perce started their walk from here.

This is where the Nez Perce planned to go.

Big Hole
(The Nez Perce rested here.)

Oregon

Idaho

Wyoming

- - - - This line shows the trail that the Nez Perce followed in order to get away from the Army.

Perhaps General Howard would get tired of chasing them and would leave them alone.

So the Nez Perce started over the mountains. The trails were rough, and the people could not go fast. The horses had a lot to carry. Now and then, some of the soldiers would catch up with them. The warriors would have to stop and fight the soldiers while the women and children and old men went on ahead.

For more than a month, the General's army chased them.

6 of 7

In late July, the tribe crossed the highest part of the Rocky Mountains. They followed a long trail down the other side toward the plains. Early in August 1877, they rested at a place called Big Hole. General Howard's soldiers were far behind them.

Chapter 8

Death at Big Hole

"If the white man wants to live in peace with the Indian, he can live in peace. There need be no trouble. Treat all men alike. Give them the same laws. Give them all an even chance to live and grow. All men were made by the same Great Spirit Chief. They are all brothers."

— Chief Joseph (Rolling Thunder)
Hin-mah-too-yah-lat-kekt

General Howard's army was not the only army that was chasing the Nez Perce. More soldiers had also come down from a fort in the north, but the Nez Perce chiefs did not know this.

Chief Looking Glass felt safe at Big Hole, so he didn't tell the warriors to guard their camp at night. He told the people to put up the teepees along a little stream. In the evening, they sang and danced together because they were still free.

Early the next morning, the soldiers attacked the Nez Perce camp.

When Proud Horse woke up, there were bullets ripping through his teepee. Gray Fox grabbed his gun and ran outside. The soldiers were already in the village, and they were shooting everyone they saw.

Proud Horse ran out to the horses. "I must keep our horses from running away," he thought to himself.

Gray Fox and the other warriors ran into the woods. The soldiers thought they had won the battle, so they began to burn the teepees.

Suddenly, Looking Glass led the warriors back to the camp. They came in from all sides and started shooting. Now it was the soldiers who were dying. Some of the soldiers ran out of the camp. The warriors chased them up a hill and trapped them behind some rocks.

Rolling Thunder took charge of the camp. "Bring the horses and pack up the camp," he called to Proud Horse and the other young men. "We must work quickly." They still had most of their horses, but they would have to leave a lot of teepees and food behind.

Proud Horse looked for his mother to tell her that she must help to load the horses. He found her lying on the ground. His brother and sister lay next to her. They were all dead.

When night came, the Nez Perce were gone. More than 70 soldiers had been killed or wounded. But 30 Nez Perce warriors and many women and children had also died at Big Hole.

For many days after that battle, the Nez Perce did not stop to rest. They knew that the white man's armies would never stop hunting them down.

Proud Horse and Gray Fox were full of sadness. They had helped to save their people, but their own family was dead.

The Nez Perce kept moving toward the plains, and the soldiers kept chasing them. The warriors fought back, but they could never stop long enough to gather food or to let the horses rest. When some of the Indians became too sick or wounded to keep going, they would stay behind and hope to die before the soldiers found them.

Chapter 9

Escape to the North

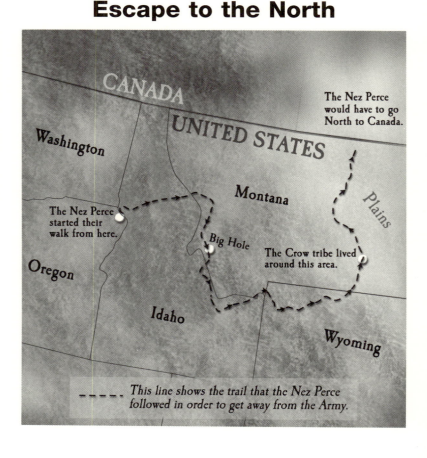

CANADA

UNITED STATES

The Nez Perce would have to go North to Canada.

Washington

Montana

The Nez Perce started their walk from here.

Big Hole

The Crow tribe lived around this area.

Plains

Oregon

Idaho

Wyoming

This line shows the trail that the Nez Perce followed in order to get away from the Army.

"The little children are freezing to death. My people — some of them have run away to the hills and have no blankets and no food. No one knows where they are — perhaps freezing to death. I want to have time to look for my children and see how many of them I can find. Maybe I shall find them among the dead."

— Chief Joseph (Rolling Thunder)
Hin-mah-too-yah-lat-kekt

Near the end of August, the Nez Perce slowed down for a few days. They had walked more than 1,000 miles. They were at the edge of the buffalo plains in Montana. "The Crow tribe lives near here," said Looking Glass. "They are our friends and they will help us," he said.

Looking Glass went on ahead to see if the Crow would join them against the Americans. But the Crow had already been beaten by the soldiers. The Crow could not help the Nez Perce now.

There was only one place left for the Nez Perce to go. They would have to go north to Canada. The Canadian border was 200 miles away. A few other Indians had already gone there to get away from the U.S. Army. Canada was outside the United States, so the U.S. Army could not go there.

"Maybe the whites in Canada will let my people live in peace," thought Looking Glass.

Looking Glass led the Nez Perce to the north. It was fall now, and cold winds were blowing across the plains.

A cold rain beat down on the horses and the people. There was not much food. Every day, more horses wore out and died.

Somehow the Nez Perce kept going. They crossed the Missouri River near a place where the army had a supply camp. At night, the Nez Perce attacked the camp and took as much food as they could carry. Then they set the camp on fire and went away.

After a few more days, the Canadian border was near.

The Nez Perce began to go slower because everyone was so tired and cold. It had begun to snow. The people wanted to stop and build fires to cook and get warm.

"There are not many horses left," said one of the chiefs. "If those horses do not rest, they will die."

The leaders argued. Looking Glass said they should rest for one night and part of the next day. He was sure that General Howard was far behind again. Another chief said that they should not stop so long.

But the people said that they were too tired to keep going.

The other chief told them, "All right. We can stop. But I think we will all be killed."

That night the tribe used branches and logs to make shelters against the banks of a big dry creek. They lit fires to cook and get warm. Proud Horse took his father's last two horses up a hill to let them graze. Then he went back to the banks of the creek to get out of the falling snow.

Proud Horse and Gray Fox were sad, but they still had hope. "There are buffalo on the plains of Canada," Gray Fox told his son. "We are almost there. Someday, Proud Horse, you can start a new family in Canada," said Gray Fox.

"We have only two horses left," said Proud Horse. "But we can start a new herd. In one or two more days, we will reach a new free land."

Chapter 10

The Last Battle

"I am tired of fighting. Our chiefs are killed. Looking Glass is dead. The old men are all dead. It is cold, and we have no blankets. The little children are freezing to death. Hear me, my chiefs! I am tired. My heart is sick and sad. From where the sun now stands I will fight no more forever."

— Chief Joseph (Rolling Thunder)
Hin-mah-too-yah-lat-kekt

It was true that General Howard was still far behind. But 400 soldiers had come from another fort in Montana. That night the scouts told the soldiers that the Nez Perce were camping only nine miles away. In the middle of the night, the soldiers got up and started riding toward the Nez Perce camp.

In the morning, Proud Horse went up on the hill to get the horses. Suddenly, he heard the sound of a bugle. He heard the thunder of guns and horses. Some of the soldiers charged toward the camp.

Other soldiers rode up the hill, shooting their guns.

Proud Horse had nothing to fight with. He jumped on a horse. He kicked its sides and yelled, and the horse ran.

When Proud Horse was far out on the plains, he stopped and looked back. He saw hundreds of Nez Perce people running across the land on foot. Soldiers and scouts were chasing the last Nez Perce horses out onto the plains. More soldiers were attacking the camp.

All that day, Proud Horse stayed out on the cold, windy plain. He could hear the shooting. He hoped that his people were winning the battle. "Maybe we will beat the Americans one last time," he thought. "If my people can take the soldiers' horses, maybe they can still get away."

But at the end of the day, he knew that this would never happen. In the last hours of light, the soldiers had surrounded the camp.

Then the sun went down.

Proud Horse began to freeze in the cold air. He hadn't eaten anything all day. His clothes were thin. His body was shaking. If he stayed out here, he would die before morning.

He began to ride back toward the camp in the dark, but his horse fell down and was too weak to get up. Proud Horse let it go. He walked toward the camp. He could see the light of the soldiers' fires.

Proud Horse crawled past the soldiers' camp and back to the creek where his people were still trapped.

Some of the warriors showed Proud Horse the body of his father. They gave him his father's gun. Proud Horse looked around. There were only about 30 men left. The horses were gone. The women were crying. Some of the warriors were singing songs. The words of the songs told them how to face death bravely.

The next morning more soldiers came. They brought more guns and a cannon. The soldiers did not charge at the Nez Perce. Instead, they just waited while the Indians froze and starved.

At noon, the soldiers shot their cannon into the camp. Then the army guns were silent again.

In the afternoon, Chief Looking Glass looked out to see what the soldiers were doing. A bullet tore off the top of his head.

Proud Horse began shooting back at the soldiers. He shot at them all day. His hands were freezing, but he shot until there were no more bullets. He never knew if he had killed any soldiers.

After a few days, General Howard arrived. Rolling Thunder carried a white flag out to him. Rolling Thunder laid down his rifle. He pointed to the sun and said, "From where the sun now stands, I will fight no more forever."

Many of his people were dead, and the rest of them became prisoners. Rolling Thunder asked for them to be sent back to the reservation. But instead they were sent to other places where many of them became sick and died.

Eight years later, in 1885, some of the Nez Perce were sent back to the tiny reservation, but Rolling Thunder was never allowed to go there.

Four years after that, in 1889, the white men broke the treaty again. They broke up the reservation and sold most of it to other white men. The Nez Perce were forced to live on an even smaller piece of land.

Proud Horse was given some land, but it was not the land of his fathers. And it would never be enough for a good herd of horses.

The End

A Note from the Start-to-Finish™ Editors

This book has been divided into approximately equal short chapters so that the student can read a chapter and take the cloze test in one reading session. This length constraint has sometimes required the authors and editors to make transitions in mid-chapter or to break up chapters in unexpected places.

You will also notice that Start-to-Finish™ Books look different from other high-low readers and chapter books. The text layout of this book coordinates with the other media components (CD and audiocassette) of the Start-to-Finish™ series.

The text in the book matches, line for line and page for page, the text shown on the computer screen, enabling readers to follow along easily in the book. Each page ends in a complete sentence so that the student can either practice the page (repeat reading) or turn the page to continue with the story. If the next sentence cannot fit on the page in its entirety, it has been shifted to the next page. For this reason, the sentence at the top of a page may not be indented, signaling that it is part of the paragraph from the preceding page.

Words are not hyphenated at the ends of lines. This sometimes creates extra space at the end of a line, but eliminates confusion for the struggling reader.